Love Blooms in Winter

By
Ruth Bawell

Table of Contents

Unsolicited Testimonials

By **Phyllis**

⭐⭐⭐⭐⭐ **Love Ruth!**

I love Ruth's books! Her mysteries are the best!

⭐⭐⭐⭐⭐ **Love This Author**

Ruth Bawell is very creative and a great writer! All her books have left me unable to stop reading till the ending! There were a few Amish fact mistakes, like unmarried man having a beard, but the plot was so good I overlooked that!

By **Steve M**

⭐⭐⭐⭐⭐ **I love romance stories** August 5, 2017
I love romance stories... well written with her usual twists to the story still enjoyed them very much Once I start I can't put it down.

By **Bones**

⭐⭐⭐⭐⭐ **Amish County Stories**
I love all the Amish County stories! Each one brings so much excitement! Ruth Bawell is also a wonderful writer!

By **Kindle Customer**

⭐⭐⭐⭐⭐ **Good clean writing.**
The Amish stories of Ruth Bawell are authentic, faith-filled writings. They are short, more the length of novellas or longer short stories. Always clean, always uplifting.

FREE GIFT

Just to say thanks for checking our works we like to gift you

Our Exclusive Never Before Released Books

100% FREE!

Please GO TO

http://cleanromancepublishing.com/gift

And get your FREE gift

Thanks for being such a wonderful client.

Chapter One

"Is this your first time on a train?" the girl opposite asked her.

Opal nodded and smiled. It felt good to see someone dressed just like her with a gown, kaap and grey shawl about her shoulders.

"I'm Maria," the girl introduced herself.

"I'm Opal Miller," Opal replied.

"You haven't taken your eyes off that window," Maria laughed.

"The countryside is beautiful," Opal said, "even though it's winter. And I'm saying goodbye to it."

"Oh, why so?" Maria asked with a sympathetic look.

"Well, I'm going to visit my aunt and cousins in Pennsylvania. They live in a village called Pinewood Grove," Opal replied.

"So it's not like you're going away forever," Maria observed.

"No. But it seems like it," Opal said with a sigh. "I don't understand why I have to be away from home at all, but I guess it's mandatory to go on Rumspringa, and for some reason, my daed thought it would be a good idea for me to go away for it."

"You must be one of the few of us who doesn't look forward to Rumspringa," Maria laughed.

"Have you had that experience?" Opal asked.

"I am still on Rumspringa," Maria replied, "and as luck would have it, I live in Pinewood Grove."

"Really?" Opal queried, incredulous.

"Yes indeed," Maria answered. "I'm traveling back from visiting my grandmother, who has been unwell." She leaned forward and patted Opal's hand. "Don't look so troubled, my dear. I will be nearby. We're bound to meet at a Sing or some other gathering."

"Thank you, Maria," Opal said gratefully. "It would certainly help to have a familiar face around." She sighed. "Though I also have my cousin Daniel there. He is on Rumspringa, and he has been asked to keep an eye on me."

"You don't sound too happy about that," Maria remarked with a smile.

"Well, Daniel is very outgoing, and I'm just a bit intimidated by that. I'm not sure that he will join the church. We hear that he is enjoying Rumspringa too much," Opal replied.

"Well," Maria said, "It's always a good thing to take Rumspringa as the opportunity that it's meant to be, to determine where you belong. There's no harm in experiencing the world and then making a choice of where one wishes to be after that."

"I know where I want to be," Opal said firmly. "Back home in Ohio, doing my chores and living a normal life in my community."

Maria smiled. "That's wonderful, Opal. To know where you belong is a step in the right direction. So now just take Rumspringa as it comes and enjoy it for what it is. And then go back to Ohio with an even greater conviction of what you believe in."

"That's good advice," Opal replied. "Thank you, Maria."

Chapter Two

Opal's aunt, Beth Miller, greeted her with a hug, then said, "I know you just arrived, but we need more flour and other provisions. Could you take the buggy out by yourself and get the things we need? You will find the people who run the mercantile are very helpful and will be happy to show you around the store so that you can find things quickly."

"Alright then," Opal said, smoothing her dress down and tucking a stray tendril of her flaxen hair under her kaap. She tried to hide her nerves, but her aunt noticed.

"Why are you looking like a frightened deer?" Mrs. Miller asked.

"I'm just not used to being out alone in Pinewood Grove yet," Opal admitted, feeling a little embarrassed.

"You'll do fine," Aunt Bet smiled. "Now, off you go. And do give the Kings our best wishes."

"Who are they?" Opal asked, looking confused.

"They own the local mercantile," Beth answered.

***

Opal entered the local Mercantile at Pinewood Grove with a certain degree of trepidation. Her Aunt Beth had sent her out with a long list of things that she needed to buy, though she did not yet know the town well.

"Can I help you?" a kindly old gentleman asked.

Opal held up the list that her aunt had given her. "My Aunt Beth and Onkel Micah send their greetings, and request you to please help me find the items on this list," Opal replied.

"And you are obviously their niece who has come all the way from Ohio," the gentleman remarked, tipping his hat. "I'm Joseph King."

Opal managed a hesitant smile. "Yes, I'm Opal Miller," she said.

"Well, Opal Miller, let's have a look at that list of yours, and see what exactly you require and if we have it all," Joseph King said cheerily.

Opal handed Joseph the list and stood by while he ran his eyes down the length of it.

"I'll show you where everything is, so that you know exactly where to find things when you're here next time," Joseph said.

Opal followed him from one section to another, piling things into her cart. She was struggling to maneuver her shopping cart out of the store when a wiry young man almost collided with her.

"I'm so sorry," Opal apologized hastily.

"Oh no, I'm sorry," the young man replied. "Here, let me help you with these."

"It's alright," Opal said hastily, "I can manage."

"No, you can't," the young man said firmly. Opal looked up, surprised, and encountered his very deep brown eyes. She turned pink with embarrassment and began to stammer out that she was quite capable of managing her own shopping, but the personable young man took the cart from her and wheeled it outside.

"I'm Samuel King, by the way," he introduced himself. "And I really should have been around to help out in the store, but I was running late today. One of our cows was unwell."

"Oh," Opal said, hurrying after Samuel.

"Where's your buggy?" he asked.

"It's right over there," Opal replied, "and I can honestly manage by myself. I don't want to trouble you."

Samuel turned to her with a smile. "Believe me, I will get into a lot of trouble with my daed if I don't see you safely into your buggy. People come to our mercantile for the excellent service they receive, and I wouldn't want to displease a customer."

"I am very happy with your store and the service," Opal said hurriedly. "And I'm sure I will shop here often, as long as I'm in Pinewood Grove."

Samuel raised his eyebrows. "Oh, I thought you lived here," he said.

"No," Opal replied, shaking her head. "I'm visiting my Aunt and Onkel... and my cousin Daniel."

"I see," Samuel said, the light of understanding in his eyes now. "You're Daniel's cousin from Ohio!"

"Yes," Opal replied. "I'm Opal Miller. Do you know Daniel?"

"Welcome to Pinewood Grove," Samuel said, "where everyone knows everyone else! To answer your question, yes, I know Daniel. And I hope you will have a very happy stay here."

"Thank you, Samuel," Opal replied. "And thank you for helping me with my shopping."

"You're welcome," Samuel replied.

"I'm sorry we didn't have as much flour as your Aunt Beth needed," Joseph said, appearing in the doorway. "But Samuel can come around with it tomorrow."

"I think Aunt Beth would be very happy about that," Opal replied gratefully.

***

"I met your friend Samuel at the mercantile," Opal told Daniel.

"Oh, you did?" Daniel remarked.

"You sound as if he's not such a good friend," Opal said with a smile.

"Oh, we are quite close. But lately, he's always lecturing me about making up my mind about joining the Church. He came to that decision after barely any Rumspringa time at all. Just because he was so quick does not mean I have to be."

"And have you made up your mind?" Opal asked, curious.

"I still have time to think about it," Daniel replied. "You see, there are aspects of the Englischer life that I do like and enjoy. Like technology."

"Hmmm…like mobile phones and televisions?" Opal queried.

"Like computers," Daniel answered, looking at her sternly. "And the freedom to access knowledge of every kind."

"To be honest," Opal said, "I haven't even begun to experience the world, and I already have the most earnest desire to stay in our Community."

"To each his own," Daniel murmured. "Anyway, I've been charged with the responsibility of showing you around Pinewood Grove, so I decided we need to break you in gently with dinner at a restaurant. Some of my friends will be there."

Opal turned pale. "But I've never been to one," she replied. Her home village was very small, and did not even have a true café. The little grocery store sold homemade pastries, but little more.

"Then it's time you did. That's a part of living in the world, and you need to experience it," Daniel said firmly.

"When do you want to do this?" Opal asked.

"This evening. I'm going to work on getting my chores done early, and you should, too," Daniel answered.

Opal nodded moodily. Then a faint glimmer of hope lifted her spirits.

"I met a really nice girl on the train," she said. "Her name is Maria. Do you know her?"

Daniel shrugged. "Can't say that I do," he replied. "Not for certain, anyway. There are more than a few Marias in Pinewood Grove, so you will have to be specific about which one you're referring to."

"I forgot to ask what her surname was," Opal sighed. "So now I can't ask you to include her in the plan for the evening. It would be nice to have another friend along."

"Don't worry," Daniel reassured Opal with a smile. "You're going to be fine."

Chapter Three

Opal picked awkwardly at her food. Daniel, who was sitting opposite her, gave her a sharp look, as if silently trying to tell her not to look so tortured. With them at the table were Daniel's friends, with whom she quickly found she had nothing in common because, though they were all Amish, they were talking about computers.

"Give us a break, Opal," Daniel said, reading her thoughts. "We've only just discovered these fascinating devices."

Opal nodded and continued to pick at her food, wishing she could catch the next train back to Ohio.

"Opal Miller?" Opal heard a familiar voice call as they walked out of the restaurant sometime later.

"Maria!" Opal exclaimed. "I was so hoping to run into you!"

"Pinewood Grove isn't a very large village," Maria grinned. "With only a couple of places to dine."

"Are you here for dinner too?" Opal asked.

Maria nodded. "But we're going to town tomorrow to see a film. Would you like to come with us?"

"I'll have to ask Daniel," Opal said.

"Where is he?" Maria asked.

"Right here," Opal replied, beckoning to Daniel to join them.

"Oh, you're the Maria that Opal has been looking for," Daniel said, coming up to them.

"Yes. We met on the train," Maria replied.

"Maria wants me to join her for a movie tomorrow," Opal announced.

"You do know you can only go if I'm with you," Daniel reminded her.

"You're most welcome to join us," Maria said quickly.

"So that's settled then," Opal said. "Right, Daniel?"

"Of course," Daniel replied, surprising Opal with his readiness to oblige.

***

"Are you going out wearing Englischer clothes?" Opal asked, looking at Daniel in surprise.

"We're going for a movie," Daniel replied. "If I dress like I usually do, I would be looked at askance, as people from our community are not usually seen at a movie theatre."

"Well, I'm going as I am," Opal said firmly. "And I'm sure Maria will too."

"Maria!" Opal exclaimed, in thinly veiled dismay when she saw Maria walking up to meet them on the sidewalk. She wore slim black leggings and a colorful top of blue and green— Englischer clothing. She looked good, but…"You look so different!"

"Yes," Maria replied with a self-deprecatory shrug. "But we're going to a movie, you know."

As they walked into the movie theatre, Opal knew what Daniel and Maria had meant. Even Maria's friends were dressed like Englischers, and some actually were Englischers, so they all merged with the crowd. But Opal felt several pairs of curious eyes on her.

"Where are you from?" a girl asked her when she and Maria were in the girls' room.

"I'm from right here in America," Opal replied, mustering a smile. "I just dress different and live differently from you. I'm Amish," she added, adjusting her kaap.

"I know you're Amish," the girl replied with a laugh. "I was asking if you were from town, because I don't ever see any Amish people in a movie theatre."

"That's because they come in disguise," Opal laughed.

"Really?" the girl replied, joining in Opal's laughter.

"Were you making fun of me?" Maria asked as she joined Opal after the movie. She sounded offended.

"No! Why?" Opal asked.

"When you made that remark about Amish people coming in disguise, it seemed like you were making fun of me," Maria replied.

"I didn't mean for it to sound like that," Opal assured her. "But I have to say that I was surprised to see you in Englischer clothes. I just thought…hoped… you would be someone who wouldn't succumb to that."

"Well, sorry to disappoint you," Maria said sharply, "but I have to do what I have to do. I want to blend in with my friends, not stand out."

She moved away from Opal then, though they made up later. But things felt different between them. And as the night wore on, Opal noticed something else. Maria appeared to like Daniel. She kept looking for reasons to stand next to him or talk to him.

"What do you think about Maria?" Opal asked Daniel later that evening.

"She's a nice person," Daniel replied.

"And do you think she looks better in Englischer clothes than in Amish clothes?" Opal queried.

"I didn't even notice. I think she's a good person. What she's wearing doesn't really matter," Daniel replied.

"Oh," Opal murmured, storing the information away. "So it doesn't alter your opinion of her in any way?" she asked.

"No," Daniel replied. "Where are you going with all these questions?"

"Nowhere in particular," Opal sighed. "But I need to have some answers, that's all."

"Look, Opal, I'm here for you if you need anything," Daniel said, suddenly serious. She was grateful for his desire to help, but she wasn't really sure what was bothering her.

"Thank you, Daniel," Opal replied. "Right now, I wish I could have help making things right with Maria. I had hoped we'd be friends, and I feel like I ruined things with that remark I made in the girls' room."

"Maria will come around, I'm sure," Daniel said.

Chapter Four

"How do you like being on Rumspringa?" Samuel asked Opal when she went around to the mercantile a few days later.

"Not very much, I'm afraid," Opal replied.

"Why, don't you like the freedom to experience the world?" Samuel quipped.

Opal flushed. "I don't think that the subject should be taken lightly," she retorted. "This is all linked to a serious decision."

"Of course," Samuel said hurriedly. "I didn't mean to cause offense. I know just how serious Rumspringa is, and how important the decision is that one needs to take eventually."

"So… do you spend all your time at the store?" Opal asked, in an effort to change the subject.

"I work on our farm, mostly," Samuel said. "That's my passion—farming. But I help Daed here in the store as well. We mill our own flour, and I package it and then bring it across to the store, along with all the produce that you see. Well, most of it."

"That's impressive," Opal replied politely.

"I do understand, you know," Samuel said after a brief silence.

"Understand what exactly?" Opal asked, struggling to keep her annoyance under control. Something about Samuel's confidence both attracted and irritated her.

"How you feel about going out and meeting different people, doing things you've never done before. Not many understand that that can be a struggle, being conflicted constantly wondering about the decision you're faced with."

"Then perhaps you don't understand me at all," Opal replied quietly. "Because I know that I don't belong out there in the world. I belong with my Community, living the simple life that I'm used to. So there's no conflict… because I have already made my decision."

Samuel folded his arms and looked down at the heavy shoes he was wearing.

"I'm sorry if I've touched a nerve, Opal, because that wasn't my intention. I know exactly how you feel because I've been there. I never wanted to have to go on Rumspringa. I love my life in the village. But I soon realized that I had to go in order to make an informed decision, one not based just on the fact that I feel comfortable here, but that this is the right thing to do, and the right place for me."

Opal looked up at Samuel just as his eyes met hers, and she held her breath for a moment.

"It's I who am sorry, Samuel," she breathed. "I didn't mean to be short with you. It's just that I'm…"

Her voice trailed off as she felt a lump in her throat.

"You don't need to explain anything to me, Opal. I understand. I really do," Samuel said softly.

"Opal! How are you today?" Joseph King said cheerily, coming up to them. "I hope Samuel has helped you find what you need."

"Oh, he has, thank you," Opal replied. "And I am very well!"

"Give my best to your Aunt and Onkel," Joseph said as Samuel picked up Opal's packages and prepared to accompany her out to her buggy.

Samuel was quiet as he and Opal piled the packages into the buggy. He tipped his hat as she climbed up and took the reins, but said nothing. Driving away, Opal hoped that she hadn't offended him in any way.

***

Samuel watched Opal's buggy drive away and gave himself a mental rap on the knuckles. He couldn't understand why he had suddenly become so tongue-tied. It was her eyes. When he had looked into them, he had seen something pure within her, and also something else. Was it realization? Fear? Surprise? He couldn't put his finger on it, except to acknowledge there was something about her that drew him. He was also acutely aware that he didn't want to say the wrong thing, and push her away.

"Nice young girl, is Opal Miller," Joseph King remarked to his son as he entered the store. "But she seemed troubled today. Is she alright?"

"She's fine," Samuel replied.

"What were you talking about?" Joseph asked.

"Nothing significant," Samuel said quickly.

"Ah," Joseph responded, and Samuel saw the twinkle in his father's eye.

"What is it, Daed?" Samuel asked. "You seem not to believe what I just said."

"You have to be a daed to know that when your son says something isn't significant, then it generally is," Joseph answered with a chuckle as he walked away. He turned around and gave

Samuel a smile. "Perhaps you could invite Opal to take a look at the farm—along with her Aunt and Onkel, of course—so that she is convinced about the quality of the produce we offer."

"Do you feel that Opal Miller doesn't trust what we sell?" Samuel asked, aghast.

"No, not at all. I just think that she is a very discerning young lady and is a regular customer, so there's no harm in reassuring her that what she purchases is organically grown and of good quality," Joseph replied. "And maybe you could ask her if she would like to put her paintings up in our store to sell."

"Paintings? What paintings?" Samuel asked, his brow wrinkled in confusion.

"Opal Miller paints some truly beautiful pictures. She spends a lot of time on it too," Joseph replied, all the while rearranging pots of preserves on a shelf.

"I had no idea," Samuel remarked. "And how do you know all this, Daed?"

"I spend all my time minding the store," Joseph laughed. "And I have a lot of time to chat with people and exchange news."

Samuel gave his father a quizzical look.

"I said I exchange news," Joseph repeated. "I don't gossip. Gossip is harmful and inaccurate.

News is that which is derived from a trusted source."

"I see," Samuel murmured, giving his father another quizzical look.

"And it would be nice to have something up in the store that's pretty and colorful," Joseph added.

"Are you sure that art will go well with preserves and produce?" Samuel asked.

"We can have a separate section for it, and maybe put in some of the tapestries and other handicrafts made in our village," Joseph replied with a firm nod.

***

"Samuel King has asked us to visit his farm," Beth announced over breakfast.

"Oh…when?" Daniel asked.

"We only need to tell him when, and he will come and fetch us," Beth replied. "He said that he and his daed are inviting their regular customers over to see how they grow their produce and also give them a tour of the farm to show them everything that's available."

"Great idea," Daniel said. "We should do that with our dairy."

"Yes, we should," Beth nodded. "But right now, we need to decide when to tell the Kings that we'd like to visit." She frowned. "Although there won't be much to see, since it's winter."

"I think it's probably to explain their farming methods to buyers, so we are assured of produce that comes from an organic source," Onkle Micah remarked.

Opal felt a tiny flutter of anticipation, but she quelled it quickly and concentrated on eating her breakfast.

"Opal, my dear," Beth said, turning to her. "Joseph King has also asked if you'd like to display your paintings in his store."

Opal looked up from her plate in surprise. "How did he know that I paint?" she asked.

"Perhaps you mentioned it?" Beth said.

"No, I didn't," Opal replied, shaking her head.

"I did," Micah Miller said, taking his glasses off his nose and placing them on the table beside his plate as he delved into his scrambled eggs.

"Oh!" Opal exclaimed in surprise.

"Joseph met me at the market and mentioned that you had just been around again to the store. I told him you were a great help at this time, when your Aunt is busy baking for the market, and that I appreciated how you found time in between all your chores and painting," Micah continued.

"That is true," Beth said, nodding.

"I also told him how good your paintings were," Micah declared. "And how visitors to the village might enjoy buying them as souvenirs of their time here."

Opal stared at her Onkel in surprise.

"I never even knew that you noticed my paintings!" she exclaimed. "And thank you for saying they are good!"

"I'm pleased, but a bit surprised that Joseph King hasn't even seen Opal's work, and yet has mentioned that he would like to display the paintings in his store. That's quite remarkable," Beth declared.

"I'll stop by at the King's farm and tell Samuel that we will visit tomorrow," Micah said, as the matter was settled.

"But I have chores," Opal said.

"We will leave when you're finished with them," Beth replied with a smile. "And perhaps you could tell Samuel that he doesn't need to trouble himself with picking us all up."

***

Opal sat in the buggy with her Aunt Beth and Daniel, and once again tried to quell the flutter she felt in her heart. She couldn't quite describe the feeling, but it was disturbing, and she wished she had a friend that she could talk to about it.

"I ran into Maria yesterday," Daniel remarked from his seat next to her.

"Oh, I wish I had been with you when you did," Opal replied.

"She said she would stop by to visit you. She felt she behaved unfairly towards you the other night and wanted to make amends."

"Oh my!" Opal exclaimed. "I'm so glad. And she's coming over? When?" Opal asked, excited.

"Tomorrow, perhaps," Daniel replied.

"Where did you run into her?" Opal queried.

"Daed and I are looking to buy more cows for the dairy farm, and her daed breeds some of the best. So that's how we met her."

Opal gave Daniel a searching look. "Maria has lived here all her life. How come you've never met her before?" she asked.

"Maybe I did meet her, and she didn't remember me," Daniel replied.

"Maybe?" Opal queried.

"Well… yes… I did," Daniel admitted. "At a Sing. But she didn't seem to notice or talk to anybody—especially not me."

"When was that?" Opal asked.

"A while ago," Daniel replied. "She looked uncomfortable. Almost like you looked at dinner the other night, and the movie."

"Maybe that's why she felt the need to dress like an Englischer," Opal mused. "To feel more comfortable and accepted. Maybe she can actually empathize with what I'm going through."

The Miller's buggy drove through the King's gate, and Opal prepared to climb down, even as Samuel appeared in the doorway and ran down the steps. He came hurrying over to help Opal down from the buggy, but she stubbornly pretended not to notice and jumped down herself, landing right in front of him. As her eyes darted up, they met his. He held her gaze for what seemed an eternity, but was no more than a mere second. It was long enough for Opal to feel like she was looking right into Samuel's heart, and what she saw there made her own heart stand still.

"Gute mariye," Samuel greeted the Millers. "Thank you all for coming to our farm. Since it's winter and we're done with the harvest, the fields look bare, but this is a good time to show you how much land we have under each crop that we grow, and what methods we use in order to get the best possible produce."

"Thank you for inviting us over, Samuel," Micah replied.

"My mamm has a meal prepared in your honor, after the farm tour," Samuel added.

"Naomi shouldn't have gone through all that trouble," Beth replied.

"Oh, she insisted," Samuel said with a light laugh.

The next hour flew by as Micah, Beth, Opal and Daniel followed Samuel on the tour he had painstakingly planned for them. He sat them down in the barn, where they sampled a variety of berries picked for the preserves that Naomi made. Opal, however, couldn't bring herself to eat anything. She felt a flutter in her heart each time she looked at Samuel. As for Samuel, it would seem that he was taking great pains to avoid even looking at her, and this made Opal rather sad. She hoped she had done nothing to offend him, and took care to listen carefully to every word he was saying. Maybe, she thought to herself, if an opportunity presented itself to her at a later stage, she would ask Samuel questions about his farm and show how genuinely interested she was in his work.

"Organic farming is difficult at times," Samuel was saying. "But it's the healthiest way to grow our food. Sometimes it's worth waiting for something to mature naturally rather than choose to rush it in any way other than nature's way."

Samuel looked briefly at Opal when he made that statement, and she wondered whether he was somehow trying to convey something to her, but she couldn't be sure. She looked away and reached for a blueberry, holding it in her hand and admiring how perfect it was.

"You must sample my mamm's preserves," Samuel said, striding over to a shelf in the barn where row upon row of jars stood, neatly labeled.

"These are ready to go out to the market," he explained, taking some jars down. Daniel sprang forward to help him, and together they carried the jars to the table where Opal was seated with Micah and Beth.

"For you… and your family," Samuel said, placing the jars of preserves before Beth.

"Thank you, Samuel," Beth said.

Later, they went into the house where Naomi King had laid out a lavish meal for them. There was a hearty, warming stew, cured ham and a basket of freshly baked bread, and blueberry pie with fresh cream to round off the spread.

"Opal, my dear, I hear you're a little homesick for Ohio?" Naomi remarked as they enjoyed the meal.

"I miss my family," Opal replied softly. "Because I've never really been away from them."

"How do you like Pinewood Grove?"

"I like it very much," Opal answered. "Everyone is so kind."

"I'm sure that when you've been here a while, you will get used to it," Naomi said.

"I don't think I will be here too much longer," Opal replied. "My mamm and daed said I was to stay just a short while, so I'm hoping to return in a couple of weeks."

"Oh, is that so?" Samuel said, looking up suddenly. And there it was again. That look. The way his eyes met hers for just the briefest of moments, and yet it seemed like she could see right into his heart.

Opal felt speech evade her, so she nodded instead.

"Thank you for this beautiful meal, Miss Naomi," she managed to say, looking away from Samuel. "I won't forget this day."

"What will you remember the most?" Naomi asked with a smile.

"The delicious blueberry pie, and learning all about updating and enhancing—but not doing away with—time-tested farming practices."

"I'm honored that you listened to me drone on," Samuel laughed.

"It interests me," Opal replied. "Anything that helps us stay with clean, honest, healthy tradition has my attention."

Naomi looked at Opal with greater interest. "I have heard a lot about you from Joseph and Samuel, but I think meeting you in person has been wonderful, Opal. I hope you will feel free to visit me at any time."

"Thank you," Opal said. "And thank you, Samuel, for taking the trouble to show us around this morning."

***

"As polite as she is lovely," Naomi remarked to her son, as they stood together watching the Millers' buggy negotiate its way out of the gate.

Samuel looked away. "I suppose I should go to the store and help Daed out."

"Things always work out the way they were meant to," Naomi said, giving her son a significant look. "Who knew that a lovely girl like Opal Miller would choose to visit our village."

"Things like that happen all the time, Mamm," Samuel said with a shrug.

Naomi patted her son on the back and walked away.

Left alone, Samuel began his now-familiar fight to get Opal Miller out of his mind. She disturbed him, and whenever she was around, he wanted to do something to impress her. He wondered if he had appeared to be making too much of an effort to impress the Millers that morning, but then it had been his daed's idea. He wondered why he was even doing things like having the Millers over… especially when Opal was going back to Ohio and indeed seemed to be in a hurry to do so. Maybe she had someone special back in her hometown.

And then it suddenly dawned on Samuel that he cared very much whether or Opal had given her heart to someone already.

"What am I thinking?" Samuel said to himself. "Opal Miller is too special a girl to be interested in the likes of me."

***

It was quiet for a while in the buggy back to the Millers' house, but then Daniel broke the silence.

"The Kings are good people," he declared. "And Samuel has changed a lot."

"He's not a young boy anymore, but a responsible man," Beth observed. "And he certainly is very capable as well, running the farm all by himself, and passionate about our beliefs."

Opal looked down at her hands folded tightly in her lap, aware that her cheeks were aflame.

"Are you alright, Opal?" Daniel asked.

"Perhaps I had a little too much blueberry pie," Opal replied with a careless laugh, still looking down at her hands.

"We must have the Kings over to our home and return their hospitality," Beth said.

"And perhaps we could invite Maria?" Opal asked hopefully. "And her family?"

"Yes," Daniel said. "Of course, we must."

Opal stared down at her hands again. She dared not meet anyone's eyes and allow them to see how excited she was about Samuel coming over.

"And when we have the Kings over," Beth said, "Opal, would you help with the meal? I think you could make your special pot roast. That will be the main dish."

"Of course," Opal said. "I'll be happy to do that."

"When will you be having the Kings and Yoders over?" Daniel asked.

"We will ask both families and see what suits them best," Micah replied.

"Opal and Daniel, don't forget the Sing tomorrow evening," Beth said suddenly. "I had almost forgotten."

"I hadn't forgotten," Opal said. "I think I rather enjoy Sings."

"I'm glad. I know that Daniel is not as enthusiastic about Sings as you are," Beth laughed.

"That's because I don't sing that well," Daniel retorted good-humoredly.

"Of course you do," Beth reassured him.

Chapter Five

The Sing was at the barn where the church services were held each Sunday, and as Opal took her seat, she glanced around the room, hoping she would see Maria. And then she did.

"Opal!" Maria greeted her. "I have been meaning to come and visit you, but I have been so busy with chores and making preserves."

Opal took Maria's hand in hers. "I'm sorry for the way I behaved that day at the movie, Maria," she said.

"No no!" Maria replied. "That was what I was going to say!"

The two girls laughed together and sat down, side by side, all their differences forgotten.

"Opal, has Daniel come with you?" Maria whispered.

"Yes, he's here, somewhere," Opal replied, giving Maria a keen look.

Maria giggled. "Ah, I suppose you've guessed," she whispered, leaning closer to Opal.

"Guessed what?" Opal asked.

"That… umm… you know… Daniel is sort of…" Maria said hesitantly.

"Oh, I knew it!" Opal exclaimed.

"Sssh," Maria said, placing a finger on her lips.

"Daniel likes you, doesn't he?" Opal whispered.

"I would have used the word interested," Maria replied.

"Have you two ever met before?" Opal asked, remembering what Daniel had told her about a Sing some time ago.

"Not formally," Maria replied. "But I remember a Sing like this one when we were both in the room, but he didn't notice me. How could he have? I was really shy and awkward."

Opal giggled. "I have a secret that I will share with you," she said. "Daniel used almost the same words when he described that Sing. He said you were there, but that you didn't notice him!"

"Oh!" Maria exclaimed. "Really? That's surprising!"

"Time to take our places," Opal said.

As Opal took her seat and looked at the row of young men facing the young girls, she drew her breath in sharply.

"Samuel…" she whispered.

There he was, right opposite her, giving her that same look that made her heart skip a beat. She didn't know that he was mesmerized by the sight of her—her cheeks aflame, the stray tendrils of hair that had escaped her kaap and caressed her cheeks, and her hands folded demurely on the table before her.

"Gut'n owed, Opal," Samuel greeted her solemnly.

"Gut'n owed, Samuel," Opal replied breathlessly.

She didn't know how she managed to hit a single note with the flutter that she had become familiar with, but Opal just knew that she didn't want the Sing to end.

"Have you decided when you're returning to Ohio?" Samuel asked as they walked out of the barn when the Sing was over.

"No," Opal answered. "I am praying over it. Whatever the Good Lord wills is what I will do."

Samuel nodded in agreement. "By the way," he said, "Your Aunt and Onkel have asked us over to lunch after Church next Sunday."

"Yes, I know," Opal replied. "We had a wonderful time at your farm, and I think Daniel would like to show you the Miller Dairy Farm."

"I would like nothing better," Samuel answered. "I'm also looking forward to seeing your paintings. Your Aunt and Onkel speak highly of your work."

"I think they're biased," Opal laughed.

"You're being modest," Samuel replied. He was quiet as they strolled outside the barn, and Opal took the opportunity to cast a veiled look at Daniel and Maria, who seemed to be getting along very well.

"Opal," Samuel said suddenly, "there's a museum in town, and it showcases a lot of our heritage. I'd like to show you around it, if I may, sometime."

Opal stared up at him, at a loss for words.

"We will, of course, ask Daniel and Maria to join us. And anyone else you would like to have come with us," Samuel added hurriedly.

"Yes!" Opal blurted out. "Yes, I'd love to see the museum." She paused. "With Daniel and Maria, of course."

"That's settled then," Samuel said, tipping his hat.

"Opal," Daniel called out. "Maria and I are joining some friends for dinner at a restaurant. Would you like to come along?"

Opal looked questioningly at Samuel.

"You must go, Opal. You're on Rumspringa, and it's always good to make your decision based on an impartial view of both sides," Samuel said.

"Would you like to come along?" Opal asked, hoping she didn't sound too eager or forward.

"I would have loved to," Samuel answered, "but I have a very early start tomorrow, and I don't want to hurry you all back on my account."

Opal nodded.

***

"Here, put this on," Maria said, handing Opal a dress.

"That's an Englischer garment," Opal said, stepping back and eyeing the dress warily.

"So it is," Maria replied. "And you're going to look very lovely in it."

"Why do you think I should wear it?" Opal asked.

"Because I think you should experience what it's like to wear clothes like these," Maria declared.

"I'm still not convinced," Opal replied.

"Just wear it," Maria urged. "It's only for a few hours. And then you can put your own familiar clothes on."

Opal put the dress on. It was sky-blue and, though modest, still revealed her legs.

She looked up to see Maria coming at her with a jar of something and strips of cloth.

"This is to make your legs look beautiful," she explained.

Opal was soon crying out in pain as Maria went to work.

"Where did you learn this form of torture?" Opal asked, her eyes filling with tears as the wax strips were applied to her legs.

"When I went out one time without doing any of this and got laughed at," Maria explained.

"Oh dear," Opal said sympathetically. "I'm sorry."

"Don't be. It taught me a few lessons," Maria declared.

"Will you stay with the Community? Or is the world beckoning to you?" Opal asked, thinking of all Maria had done to blend in with the Englischers.

"I haven't made up my mind yet," Maria said. "I'm being honest."

"What about Daniel? Do you think he will want to live out in the world too?" Opal queried.

"He's attracted by the technology and all the possibilities it opens up," Maria said.

"If he really likes you and you choose the world, then Daniel will follow, won't he?" Opal remarked anxiously.

Maria bit her lip. "I'm sorry, Opal. I can't answer that question. Anyway, hurry and put these shoes on and let's go," she said, helping Opal slide her feet into a pair of pumps. Then Opal quickly brushed out her waist-length hair that now hung loosely about her shoulders, and they were ready to go.

"I don't feel like myself," Opal said, thinking longingly of the Sing earlier. Somehow this whole experience of dressing to go out to dinner was succeeding only in detracting from the charm of those moments. She remembered sitting opposite Samuel and occasionally looking into his eyes and reading all that remained unspoken within them.

"How are we going?" Opal asked as she brought her thoughts back to the evening ahead.

"Daniel has booked a cab," Maria said, just as a large cab drove up and stopped in front of the Millers' gate.

"I'm glad my Aunt Beth didn't see me in this dress," Opal remarked, as they climbed into the cab.

"Mamm was probably watching you discreetly from behind the curtains as you stepped out, Opal," Daniel laughed. "But this is Rumspringa, so you're okay!"

The restaurant turned out to be a pub, and Opal immediately began to panic.

"I think I should go home," she said.

"No," Maria replied firmly. "You're going to stay here and experience what this world is all about. None of us is going to indulge in any alcohol anyway. We just like the music here."

"You've been before, haven't you?" Opal asked.

"Yes," Daniel replied.

They were joined by more of Daniel's and Maria's friends, and Opal withdrew further.

She was unaware of how attractive she looked in her sky-blue dress and long, blonde hair. She wore just the barest hint of makeup, and her eyes were filled with an innocence and purity that few around there possessed.

It was not long before a young man approached her with a glass.

"May I get you a drink?" he asked.

"No, thank you," Opal responded politely, noticing that Daniel had abandoned her and gone off with Maria. They were now with another group of people, laughing and conversing. She felt instantly alienated from both of them and her surroundings, and turned to go.

"Hey, don't go," the young man said.

"This type of place isn't really for me," Opal replied, trying to be polite.

"Well, let's help you feel at home, in that case. I'm Peter. What's your name?"

"Opal Miller," Opal replied hesitantly.

"You're very beautiful," Peter remarked.

"Thank you, but I'm not myself today. You should see me when I am," Opal retorted.

"Ah, a sense of humor. I like that in a girl," Peter said.

"I really do have to leave now," Opal said. "Could you help me book a cab, please?"

"Sure," Peter replied, walking out of the pub with her.

"Opal!" she heard a familiar voice exclaim. She looked up to see Samuel staring at her, almost in horror. He was wearing his traditional Amish clothes, of course, and Opal suddenly felt very awkward. "What happened to you?"

"Who's this?" Peter asked. "He's dressed very formally for the likes of this place."

"Samuel," Opal said, ignoring the young man's remark. "I'm glad to see you. I need to get home, and Peter was just helping me with a cab."

"Peter?" Samuel asked uncomprehendingly.

"Yes," Opal answered, introducing Peter to Samuel.

"Why don't we all go back inside the pub and enjoy the rest of the evening?" Peter suggested.

"No, thank you. I think I'd like to go home," Opal replied politely. She turned to Samuel. "Would you please drive me?" she asked, and followed him when he nodded silently.

Samuel remained quiet as he walked Opal to his buggy and helped her in. Opal felt her heart plummet. He hadn't looked at her the way he had earlier in the evening at the Sing, and she knew that she had disappointed him in some way.

"I know it's none of my business, but why the Englischer clothes?" Samuel asked.

"You recommended that I go and experience the world, and that's exactly what I was doing," Opal replied hotly, trying to disguise her distress.

"You could have gone somewhere else. A coffee shop maybe—or anywhere where you didn't have to lose your identity completely," Samuel shot back.

"I haven't lost my identity, Samuel," Opal said. "And I was trying to find my way home."

"With a strange man," Samuel said, almost angrily.

"Well, Daniel had taken off and was with his friends. Maria was with him. I was all alone and I just felt terrible. Then Peter came along, and I asked him to help me find a cab."

"Well, I'll get you home," Samuel said, and fell silent after that.

"Thank you for bringing me back," Opal said gratefully as they arrived at her aunt and onkle's house. She stepped out of the buggy and looked up at Samuel, wishing he had helped her down.

Samuel acknowledged Opal's thanks with a nod and drove away rapidly. Opal stood watching his buggy, overwhelmed by a feeling of abject despair, and then turned to go inside.

She slipped up to her room, hurriedly changed into her nightclothes, and braided her hair… wishing all the while that Maria hadn't persuaded her to wear the Englischer dress. It was obvious that it had displeased Samuel and caused him to view her differently. Contempt would be too strong a word, Opal decided, but perhaps disappointment might well describe Samuel's attitude towards her that evening.

She couldn't help crying herself to sleep. She was homesick, and now she was also burdened with the lost hope of Samuel ever looking at her the way he had before.

Chapter Six

Opal bustled about the kitchen helping Beth prepare the meal for the Kings and Yoders. She had hurried back from church to put the finishing touches on her pot roast. But instead of being excited about the upcoming dinner, she struggled to keep her tears down as she remembered how Samuel had sat stoic, not casting a single look in her direction through the whole of the service that morning. It was therefore with a sense of relief that she peeped out of the kitchen window to see a buggy pull up and Samuel emerge with his parents. She had worried that he might not even come.

Moments later, the Yoders arrived too.

"Come out, Opal," Beth said, stepping into the kitchen and urging her niece out.

"But the vegetables aren't done yet, Aunt Beth," Opal protested.

"I'll take care of those," Beth said. "You go on out and attend to our guests with Daniel.

Opal went into the living room where their guests were seated. Micah was regaling them with details about the Miller Dairy, and Opal slipped in and hoped nobody would notice her.

"Here's my niece, Opal," Micah said. "You've met her, of course."

"We haven't had the pleasure," Maria's mother Elizabeth declared. "But I've heard all about you from Maria. And we have just been admiring your paintings."

Opal nodded and smiled at Elizabeth and Maria's father, Ezekiel. She cast a glance in Samuel's direction, but he didn't look up and meet her eyes as she hoped he would. Well, that chapter was closed, Opal thought to herself.

"Lunch is ready," Beth announced as she came into the living room, and Opal hurried away to help her.

As the men seated themselves, the womenfolk served them and then sat down at another table. Opal was glad that she didn't have to make any conversation with Samuel.

"Opal made the pot roast," Beth announced. "Isn't it delicious?"

Naomi King immediately heaped compliments on Opal, and Elizabeth Yoder followed suit. But Opal kept her eyes fixed on her plate and barely touched her food.

After lunch, everyone followed Micah to the dairy sheds that he and Daniel were eager to show off. Opal hung back, saying she would do the washing up, but Beth wouldn't hear of it. David and Maria walked together, and Opal felt a twinge of envy.

"They seem to be getting along really well," Opal heard someone remark. She looked up, surprised. It was Samuel.

"Yes," she said, her heart pounding.

"I owe you an apology," Samuel said, slowing down so that the two of them were well behind the others.

"Whatever for?" Opal asked, feigning innocence of anything that could possibly have offended her.

"For my behavior the other night. I was out of line," Samuel answered.

"Oh, that's alright," Opal replied, feeling relief sweep over her.

"I went home and thought about my reaction to seeing you in that dress," Samuel continued. "I like being honest with myself... and now, with you. You looked devastatingly beautiful, Opal. And it frightened me. I didn't want some other lucky man to earn your attention or your heart. I so desperately wanted that lucky man to be me."

"I don't understand what you mean," Opal blurted out. "I thought you were disgusted by how I looked!"

"Far from it," Samuel said, stopping to face her. The others wandered into one of the dairy sheds, leaving them alone. "I was blinded by the sight of you, and for one moment, I wished for something else—another life, a different world. I was so conflicted."

"Samuel, slow down," Opal said. "You're not making any sense."

"I am, Opal. For the first time, I could see myself like I never have before. I thought I was clear about what I wanted. But seeing you dressed like that, so blindingly beautiful, with your hair like liquid gold…"

Samuel paused.

"What is it, Samuel?" Opal queried. "Please tell me what you're trying to say, but aren't."

"You used to be Opal Miller in a gown and kaap, but I saw a different Opal, and that version of you disturbed me. Now I will always think of that Opal, and it will lead me away from what I want and where I want to be. So Opal, though I so hoped I might come to your Aunt and Onkel and formally ask to court you, I have decided that it won't be the best course for me."

"That's... that's... preposterous!" Opal exclaimed, for want of any other word to describe what she was feeling. "You don't mean that, Samuel!"

"I do, I'm afraid," Samuel said. "Please think kindly of me when you're back in Ohio. And I will try not to remember you as you looked that night when I found you with a stranger trying to find your way home."

Opal gave Samuel a look of utter bewilderment.

"I think I'll go and wash the dishes," she said, and hurried away.

***

"What happened between you and Samuel?" Beth asked later. "I thought you both were getting along well. I have to admit, your Onkel and I were trying to do all we could to make sure you both got to know each other."

"I'm sorry, Aunt Beth," Opal apologized. "Samuel seems a little confused about a few things. And as for me, I just need to get myself home."

Chapter Seven

"You're not going back already, are you?" Maria asked the next day. Opal had sought out her friend to tell her goodbye before leaving.

"I am," Opal replied. "I'm happy for you and Daniel, by the way."

"Yes," Maria smiled. "He has asked to court me."

"That's wonderful," Opal remarked. She tried to force some enthusiasm into her voice, but was unable to quell a large twinge of regret at her own misfortune.

"I shouldn't have worn that dress that night," she declared sadly.

"I'm sorry. I heard that Samuel wasn't too pleased," Maria said.

"He said it confused him about what he wants," Opal sighed.

"Talking of being confused," Maria said, "Daniel and I have made a decision finally… to remain in the Community."

"What wonderful news!" Opal said, hugging her friend. "I'm so happy for you."

"You helped us, Opal. You were always so sure of where you wanted to be," Maria replied.

"Well, I'm glad you both found each other," Opal remarked. She thought how ironic it was that the two who were most certain of where they wanted to be were Samuel and her. But now it seemed that Daniel and Maria's lives were falling into place, while hers and Samuel's were falling apart.

***

"Are you ready, Opal?" Micah Miller called. "I'll take you to the station. Give me a minute while I fetch the buggy."

"I'll wait right here, Onkel Micah," Opal said, standing by the porch with her suitcase beside her. She heard voices towards the barn, and turned to look just in time to see Onkel Micah rush inside the large building.

Moments later, she saw Daniel race past her looking distressed.

"What's going on?" Opal shouted out.

"One of the cows is in labor," Daniel shouted back. "And it's complicated. Daed is there with her."

"But he's supposed to be dropping me to the station to catch my train home," Opal cried.

"I'm running to the phone booth now to try and call for a cab to take you," Daniel called out, and disappeared.

As Opal stood waiting, it began to snow just as Daniel returned, breathless. "The good news is, the train won't depart on schedule because of the snow. The bad news is that there are no cabs available at the moment, so you'll have to wait a little longer," he said.

"How is your cow?" Opal asked, turning her mind from her own problems.

"In a great deal of pain, I gather. And I need to get to her now and help Daed out," Daniel replied.

"Maybe I should reschedule my departure," Opal said.

"Don't worry," Daniel replied. "I'll go back to the phone booth and try to call a cab as soon as I've helped Daed deliver the calf."

Opal picked up her suitcase. She didn't want to miss her train. She was determined to get to the station and sit on the train even if it didn't move until the next day. She just needed to get away.

As if in answer to her silent prayer, a cab came through the gate just then.

"I got a call from my agency," the driver said. "They asked me to come here."

"Yes," Opal answered, relieved. "I need to be dropped to the train station."

As the cab sped away from the Millers' house, Opal looked back with a pang. Her Aunt Beth was on the porch waving to her, but Daniel and her Onkel Micah were still with the cow. Opal was thinking of all the good times she had had with this part of her extended family, but when she thought of Samuel, her eyes filled with tears.

"The snow's coming down heavily," the cab driver remarked.

"Yes, I know," Opal replied. "But I have to get to the station."

They were almost out of Pinewood Grove by then, and Opal was beginning to feel a sense of excitement at going back home.

"I'm sorry, lady," the cab driver said suddenly. "I think I made a huge mistake in agreeing to come and fetch you. We need to turn back now."

"Please," Opal begged. "I can't go back. I just need to get home. Catching that train is of the utmost importance."

"It might be, but consider my situation. I can barely see a few feet ahead, and your life is in as much danger as mine in such extreme weather."

As if the weather were giving a sign of agreement, a tree dropped a branch right in their path.

"Oh my!" Opal exclaimed. The driver pulled up just in time. Turning around, he tried to soothe Opal.

"Don't worry. We'll find a way to shelter. We don't want to stay in the cab all night."

"I'm dreadfully sorry," Opal apologized tearfully. "How far is it to the station? I will proceed on foot."

"And leave me with a dead girl on my conscience?" the driver scolded. "Not on your life. You keep seated, lady, until I get us somewhere safe."

"Where will we go?" Opal asked, beginning to panic. The winds had picked up, and the snow was coming down much harder and faster.

"Wherever I can get to in this snow," the driver replied.

Opal tried not to burst into tears, gripping her seat firmly as the driver struggled to get through the snow.

"Well, this is as far as we go," the cab driver declared. "I'm calling for help now, and whoever comes will take you back to Pinewood Grove. This is no time to be out on the road, even if you have a seat booked on a train.”

“How far would you say the train station is?” Opal asked.

“Why are you asking? You’re surely not contemplating walking there?” the driver asked, aghast.

Opal swallowed. “I am,” she admitted.

“Well, I won’t let you, lady, and it’s for your own good,” the cab driver declared.

“You can’t hold me hostage,” Opal protested. She knew she was overreacting, but her nerves were beginning to fray.

“I’m not holding you hostage,” the driver said calmly. “I’m just looking out for you.”

Suddenly, out of the wall of snow, a dark shape appeared—a buggy!

“Help!” Opal cried, leaping out of the cab into the snow. “Help! Please!”

The buggy stopped, and Opal saw a horse covered in snow, shaking snowflakes from its mane.

“Help!” she cried louder, and the cab driver joined her.

“Opal!” a familiar voice called out. Opal began to sob.

"Samuel! Samuel! Am I dreaming? Is it you?" she cried.

"Opal! It's me!" Samuel replied, hurrying forward and making deep indentations in the snow with his boots. "What happened?"

"The snow stopped our progress," the cab driver explained. "And this young woman has a train to catch."

Samuel rushed towards Opal and took her hands in both of his.

"You're freezing," he said. "I'm going to get you back to the Millers'."

"I'm on the way to the station," Opal said. "I have to go home."

"Not today you aren't," Samuel said firmly. "I'll tow you to the side of the street," he said to the cab driver.

"How?" the driver said.

"You haven't heard of horsepower, have you?" Samuel laughed, hitching the horse to the taxi and maneuvering it so that the cab was soon free of the snow. When they had it safely on the side of the street, Samuel had the cab driver climb into his buggy along with Opal, and they headed back to Pinewood Grove.

**

Later, back at the Millers' house by the fire, Opal looked at Samuel.

"How did you find me?" she asked.

"Well, I actually came to say goodbye, and I was told you had already left. I needed to say something to you before you left, so I followed."

"What did you want to say?" Opal asked.

"I will tell you later, I think. Right now, you stay warm by the fire," Samuel said. "I heard that Daniel and your Onkel are still with the cow. I'm going to help."

"Come dear," Beth said to her niece. "Eat something. You need to keep your strength up."

Opal looked sadly at Beth. "I missed the train, Aunt Beth."

"Luckily, it's not the last train that goes to Ohio," Beth laughed. "Now cheer up, child, and thank the Good Lord for sending Samuel to rescue you."

Opal seated herself at the table with the cab driver and her Aunt and ate the meal laid out for them.

Some time later, Micah and Daniel came in.

"Where's Samuel?" Beth asked.

"The cow delivered, finally!" Micah announced. "Samuel is with the mother and the newborn."

"Would you like to go out to the dairy shed and take a look at the newborn?" Beth asked Opal.

Opal nodded.

"Well then, put your warm cloak on and take this umbrella," Beth instructed. "And come back quickly."

"I will," Opal replied, gratefully accepting the opportunity for a few minutes alone with Samuel.

Chapter Eight

"Samuel," Opal said, standing in the doorway of the dairy shed.

"Opal," Samuel whispered, not taking his eyes off the calf before him. "Look at this little one. Isn't he a beauty?"

"Yes," Opal said, kneeling down by Samuel's side and admiring the newborn calf.

She could feel Samuel's eyes on her.

"What is it that you wanted to say to me earlier?" Opal asked, bringing them back to their brief moment together in the kitchen.

"I just wanted to say I was wrong, and that I made a huge mistake," Samuel replied with a sigh.

"Oh?" Opal murmured.

"Yes," Samuel answered. "After some more soul searching, I realized that I was disturbed by how beautiful you looked that night, because I did want a different life. A life with you forever. And seeing you like that, with that strange man, I remembered how my sister left the community for an Englischer. I suppose I pushed you away because I didn't want to feel that kind of pain again, in case you too decided not to remain with the Community.

"I understand," Opal said. "But I didn't know you had a sister."

"We don't talk of her," Samuel said. "And there's something else. I was afraid to face my feelings and my fear that you might turn me down if I asked to court you," Samuel admitted.

"What caused your change of heart?" Opal asked.

"Hearing you had left for the train station alone," Samuel said. "I already knew I had feelings for you, Opal, but hearing you had gone off all by yourself filled me with the kind of pain I never want to feel again."

Samuel took her hand in both of his. "You are strong yet vulnerable, and I have wanted to protect you from the first moment I set eyes on you. I never want to see you sad. I guess those feelings frightened me, so I fear I drove you away."

Opal looked down at her hand in Samuel's.

"While we were delivering the calf, I had the opportunity to ask your Onkel Micah for permission to court you," Samuel continued. "If you will allow me to, of course."

Opal grinned with delight. But before she could answer, she heard a familiar voice. She sat back on her heels. "There's something happening outside," she remarked, getting to her feet. "I hear voices. Beloved voices!"

At that moment, the shed door opened and Opal saw her own mamm and daed standing there.

"Mamm! Daed! What are you doing here?" Opal cried in delight.

"Your sister and brother are inside the house, but we had to come and find you," Opal's mother said. "Oh, Opal!" She continued. "Your Aunt Beth wrote to tell us you were homesick so we decided to visit. And we just heard what happened in the snow!"

Samuel stood up and tipped his hat respectfully to Opal's parents, who glanced curiously at him.

"You didn't tell us you were coming, and I was to leave on the train today and go home!" Opal exclaimed.

"We heard," Opal's mother said. "We're grateful to the Good Lord for stopping you!"

"And to this good young man for rescuing you," Opal's father cut in.

"Micah said that there was something you wanted to ask us," he added, looking enquiringly at Samuel.

"There is," Samuel replied. "I would like your permission to court your daughter."

Opal looked from her father to Samuel and smiled. The look in his eyes told her all she needed to know.

"Rumspringa is officially over," she said. "And I have made my decision."

"For you, it was over before it even began," Samuel laughed. "Just as my heart was yours the first time I saw you."

The End

FREE GIFT

Just to say thanks for checking our works we like to gift you

Our Exclusive Never Before Released Books

100% FREE!

Please GO TO

`http://cleanromancepublishing.com/gift`

And get your FREE gift

Thanks for being such a wonderful client.

Please Check out My Other Works

By checking out the link below

http://cleanromancepublishing.com/rbauth

Thank You

Many thanks for taking the time to buy and read through this book.

It means lots to be supported by SPECIAL readers like YOU.

Hope you enjoyed the book; please support my writing by leaving an honest review to assist other readers.

.

With Regards,

Ruth Bawell